Jesse's Daycare

AMY VALENS

Illustrated by Richard Brown

Houghton Mifflin Company
Boston 1990

For Lynn, Judy, Tona, Leslie, and Gabi,
who opened their homes and
their hearts to my son
— A.V.

Library of Congress Cataloging-in-Publication Data

Valens, Amy.
   Jesse's daycare/Amy Valens; illustrated by Richard Brown.
      p.   cm.
   Summary: Compares the daily events of mother and son as one goes
to work and the other goes to day care.
   ISBN 0-395-53357-0
   [1. Day care centers—Fiction. 2. Parent and child—Fiction.]
I. Brown, Richard Eric, 1946– ill. II. Title.
PZ7.V227Je   1990   89-24507
[E]—dc20   CIP
                           AC

Printed in the United States of America

WOZ   10 9 8 7 6 5 4 3 2 1

.

When Jesse's mom goes to work, she brings
Jesse to daycare at Sara's house.

Sometimes just he and Sara are there.

Sometimes there are other kids, too.
Sara's mom takes care of them all.

Jesse doesn't like to leave his mother.
It makes him feel sad.

His mom is sad to leave Jesse, too.
"See you this evening, Jesse!" she says.

Sara's mom understands how Jesse feels.

She reads Jesse and Sara
a story while Jesse's mom drives to work.

At first, Jesse is too sad to play with Sara,
even though she's his friend.

When Jesse's mom gets to work,
she says "Hi" to her friends.

Sara takes out her toy cars.
Jesse loves toy cars!

Now he is ready to play.
He doesn't feel sad anymore.

Jesse and Sara are busy all morning!

Jesse's mom is busy all morning, too,
doing her job.

At snack time, Jesse and Sara eat
apples and oranges.

Jesse's mom likes a cup of tea
when she takes her break.

Jesse shows Sara how to make
a cake out of sand.

Jesse's mom shares what she knows
with other people, too.

Jesse has a good time at daycare, but
he still misses his mom sometimes.

Jesse's mom misses him, too.

On some days she calls
at lunch time to say "Hi!"

At nap time, Jesse sleeps with his bear.

His mom wishes she had a nap time,
too, but she still has work to do.

In the afternoon, Jesse and Sara
help in the kitchen.

On nice days, Sara's mom
takes them for a walk.

When she's through with work, Jesse's
mom drives to Sara's house to take Jesse home.

Some days, Jesse is having so much fun at daycare, he's surprised when his mom comes!

Jesse doesn't want to leave.

His mom helps him put on his jacket.

"You can come back tomorrow, Jesse."

Sara and her mom say, "Goodbye, Jesse!"
"Goodbye," says Jesse. "See you tomorrow."

On the way home, Jesse and his mom tell
each other all about their day.

E
Valens, Amy.
Jesse's daycare
793-1395